My **Daddy** Has **PTSD**

Illustrated
ory Book
Help
ildren
derstand
st-Traumatic
ess
sorder

e publishing
ILDREN'S DIVISION

by Casey Sean Harmon

Published by Tate Publishing & Enterprises, LLC
127 E. Trade Center Terrace | Mustang, Oklahoma 73064 USA
1.888.361.9473 | www.tatepublishing.com

Tate Publishing is committed to excellence in the publishing industry. The company reflects the philosophy established by the founders, based on Psalm 68:11,
"The Lord gave the word and great was the company of those who published it."

Book design copyright © 2015 by Tate Publishing, LLC. All rights reserved.
Cover and interior design by James Mensidor
Illustrations by Louise Pulvera

Published in the United States of America

ISBN: 978-1-63449-805-0
Juvenile Nonfiction / Health & Daily Living / General
14.11.27

To Liam

Introduction

I wrote My Daddy Has PTSD for my son shortly after I was diagnosed with PTSD. It became apparent to me that PTSD is a subject many people try to avoid because so few people understand what it is. That is the wrong answer. People need to understand, and it needs to start with our children.

During my seven-year tour on a Unit Ministry Team in the U.S. Army, I witnessed things that few people can imagine—things that will last in my memory forever. From having to bury a battle buddy who committed suicide in front of his wife and kids, to witnessing the last breath of two of my battle buddies following a tragic vehicle accident. And yet as traumatic as these things were, the hardest part was providing support to the family members and battle buddies who were left behind. Over the years, I have dealt with (or helped to deal with) hundreds of cases pertaining to suicides, combat deaths, post-traumatic stress, and marriage/family counseling for soldiers, veterans, and family members. So when I was diagnosed with

PTSD, I knew exactly what I was dealing with. I also knew that my loving family would have to suffer right alongside me.

So I wrote this book as a tool to help explain to my son exactly what it is that Daddy is dealing with. I believe that plenty of other daddies (and mommies too) can also use this book to help explain their symptoms to their children.

The subject of PTSD is very near and dear to my heart. I have seen the problems that trauma-caused anxiety, depression, stress, and fear can create with soldiers and their family members. I have heard the cries and witnessed the destruction. This disorder is very real, and more common than you may think.

In conclusion, I would like to state that behind every good soldier is a good family. We could not do what we do without the support of our loved ones. Thanks!

Hooah!

SGT Casey S. Harmon, 2014

When my daddy got back from the war, my whole family was happy to see him. I could tell something was wrong with Daddy because he was quiet and his hands would shake for no reason. I don't remember Daddy's hands shaking for no reason before he left.

Mama says that my daddy has PTSD. She says it causes daddy to be nervous and to do things without realizing it. She says he picked it up from the war.

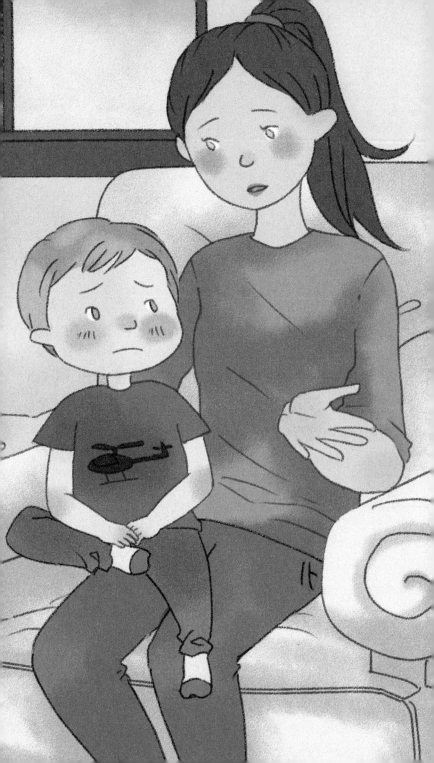

I can tell the PTSD is bothering Daddy. The other day, he fell to his knees when he heard a car backfire. I heard it too, but I didn't fall to my knees. Daddy looked very scared.

When we went to the commissary, Daddy had to leave Mama and me because he said that there were too many people around. Me and Mama go to the commissary all the time. I never noticed there were too many people.

I accidentally dropped a spoon in the kitchen when Mama was pouring my cereal. Daddy got mad and yelled at me. He said that I shouldn't be so clumsy. I was afraid, because I had never heard Daddy yell like that before. After a minute, he gave me a hug and said he was sorry for yelling.

Daddy decided that he should go see a counselor, so Mama and me went with him. The counselor told us that Daddy would be okay, and that Mama and me would have to do things to help Daddy deal with his PTSD. I said that I would help Daddy, because I love him.

When we got back home, Daddy told me that he saw some ugly things in the war. He said that loud noises remind him of the noises he heard over there. He also said that large crowds of people make him feel unsafe. I knew that this was all because of the PTSD, and I wanted to help Daddy get better.

While Daddy was driving, I saw that his face was beginning to sweat very badly. I tapped Mama from the backseat and whispered, "I think the road is scaring Daddy." Mama looked at Daddy and said, "It's okay. There's nothing to be afraid of." Daddy smiled and took Mama's hand. He said, "Thank you."

Later, Daddy and me went to the park to feed the ducks. In the parking lot, a motorcycle drove by, and it was very loud. Daddy stopped walking, and I could tell the noise bothered him. I reached out and took his hand. "It's all right," I told my daddy. "I'm right here."

Daddy smiled. He wiped his eyes and said, "Thank you for being there for me."

I can tell Daddy is doing better since me and Mama have been helping. I'm glad that my daddy made it back from the war, and that he will be okay.

Afterword

So what exactly is PTSD? According to the U.S. Department of Veterans Affairs: "PTSD, or Post-traumatic Stress Disorder, is a psychiatric disorder that can occur following the experience or witnessing of a life-threatening event such as military combat, natural disasters, terrorist incidents, serious accidents, or physical or sexual assault in adult or childhood."

How does PTSD affect children? According to FamilyOfaVet.com, a website devoted to helping veterans and family members cope with PTSD and TBI (Traumatic Brain Injury): "Military and veteran families are at risk of developing secondary PTSD. Children in these families are exposed to stress levels that could be considered toxic, according to The American Academy of Pediatrics. The National Center for Child Traumatic Stress notes that, 'Military children experience unique challenges related to military life and culture. These include deployment-related stressors and reintegration.' Military children live with the constant fear of losing a parent, parental separation, moving and making new friends, all while living in a household with one often overloaded parent holding down the fort. The dynamics of welcoming a returning parent that has been injured physically or mentally is real. Children often mimic behaviors of a returning parent with

Post-Traumatic Stress Disorder. Even an at-home parent struggling with anxiety can have a significant impact on their children's wellbeing. Managing stress as a family needs to be a high priority."

Communication is key when it comes to coping with symptoms of PTSD. It is important for those who suffer to open up to their children so that they are not left to speculate. Often, children who are left in the dark about such things either blame themselves for the negative actions of their parent(s), or they tend to mimic the actions of their parent(s)—not realizing that the actions are unhealthy. It is important for children to understand that the things that PTSD sufferers go through are not their fault—it's the PTSD. Some things that parents can do to help their children understand are: explain to them what PTSD is, and (without going into too much detail) how it affects you; read to them books that are written by, or about, other people who suffer from PTSD so that they know that you (and they) are not alone; and spend a lot of quality time with them so that they know that, despite your PTSD, you still love and care for them. These simple things can make a world of difference to everyone involved.

Please be sure to tell someone
about this book today!

e|LIVE

listen|imagine|view|experienc‹

AUDIO BOOK DOWNLOAD INCLUDED WITH THIS BOOK!

In your hands you hold a complete digital entertainment package. In addition to the paper version, you receive a free download of the audic version of this book. Simply use the code listed below when visiting our website. Once downloaded to your computer, you can listen to the book through your computer's speakers, burn it to an audio CD or save the file to your portable music device (such as Apple's popular iPod) and listen or the go!

How to get your free audio book digital download:

1. Visit www.tatepublishing.com and click on the e|LIVE logo on the home page.
2. Enter the following coupon code:
   a8bd-559d-ffc8-38f2-daf9-aadf-44ca-5baf
3. Download the audio book from your e|LIVE digital locker and begin enjoying your new digital entertainment package today!

CPSIA information can be obtained
at www.ICGtesting.com
Printed in the USA
LVOW02s1910041116
511687LV00005B/28/P